Why C

Fold Your

David Levine?

Why Can't You Fold Your Pants Like David Levine?

by Frieda Wishinsky
pictures by Jackie Snider

A Ready ☆ Set ☆ Read® Book

HarperCollins*PublishersLtd*

Produced by Caterpillar Press

Ready ☆ Set ☆ Read is a registered trademark of
HarperCollins Publishers Ltd

Canadian Cataloguing in Publication Data

Wishinsky, Frieda
Why can't you fold your pants like David Levine?

"A ready set read book".
ISBN 0-00-223994-9

I. Snider, Jackie. II. Title.

PS8595.I85W5 1993   j813'.54   C93-094618-9
PZ7.W5Wh 1993

For my best friend, Bill
Frieda

For Stephen
Jackie

Nothing was ever

good enough for

Stanley's mother.

On Monday,

Stanley got a 90

in math and ran home

to tell his mother.

“Mom, I got a 90 in math!”

he exclaimed.

“90 isn’t bad dear.

Of course, 100 would

have been better.”

On Tuesday,

Stanley played in the

biggest baseball game

of the season.

He hit a home run

in the ninth inning

and won the game

for his team.

"Oh boy!" thought Stanley,

as he ran home to

announce the news.

But before he could

get out a word,

his mother said, "Look at you.

You're covered in mud.

Why can't you ever stay clean?"

That night at dinner,

Stanley ate

two hamburgers

and all of his peas.

He tried eating his beets,

but they wouldn't go down.

"I ate all those peas,"

he thought, "a few beets

won't matter."

"May I have some dessert,

Mom?" he asked,

eyeing the cherry pie.

"Finish your beets or

no dessert,"

she said firmly.

On Saturday afternoon,

Mrs. Levine and

Mrs. Perkins came over

for coffee.

Stanley agreed to

play the violin, and wore

his best pants

and a new blue shirt.

When everyone was seated,

he lifted the bow and played

‘Flight of the Bumblebee’

with only two mistakes.

"You are talented, dear,"

said Mrs. Perkins.

"You have artistic hands,"

said Mrs. Levine.

"You need more practice,"

said Stanley's mother.

That night,

before Stanley went to bed,

he put his pants on the chair.

Then he climbed into bed

and waited for his mother.

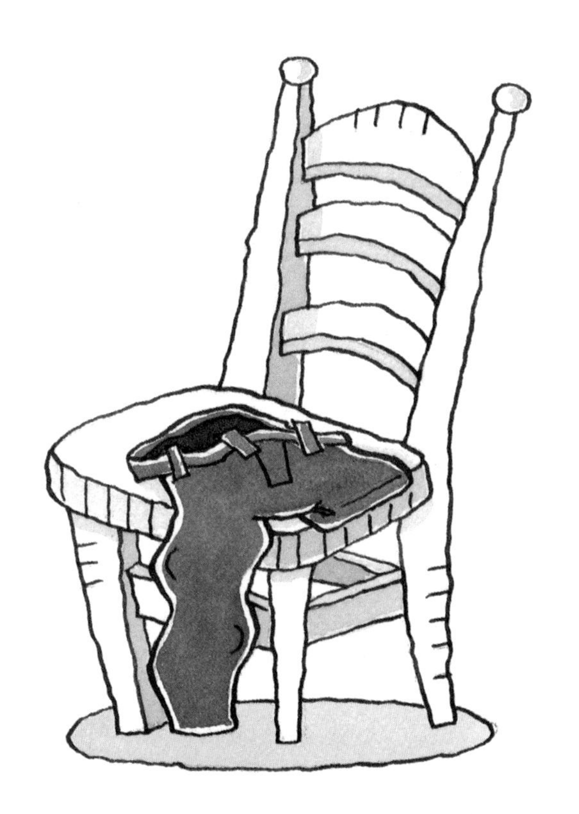

“Stanley,” she said, when
she came into the room.
“You’ve folded your pants
all wrong. Why can’t you
fold your pants like David Levine?
Mrs. Levine says that
David takes such good
care of his clothes.”

Stanley had enough.

Early the next morning,
he stuffed his clothes,
his violin and some food
into a pillowcase.
He scribbled a note
to his mother.

It said:

Dear Mother,

If you like David Levine
so much, why don't you
adopt him? I'm going
someplace where I'll be
more appreciated.

Your son,

Stanley

Stanley opened the

front door

and began to walk.

The streets were quiet.

No one was up.

He passed the park.

He sat down on

an empty bench and

dug into his pillowcase.

But before he could

take anything out,

someone called his name.

It was David Levine.

"What are you doing here?"

Stanley asked.

“I’m walking my dog,”

said David.

“What are *you* doing here?”

Stanley ignored

the question.

"I hear you're pretty good

at folding pants,"

said Stanley.

David's glasses slipped

down his nose.

"What do you mean?"

he asked, pushing up

his glasses.

“Your mother has been

bragging about how

perfect you are,”

said Stanley.

"Well, all I hear is

how talented you are.

My mother wants me to

play the violin just like you."

"Are you kidding?"

asked Stanley.

"I wouldn't kid

about the violin,"

said David.

For a minute

the boys were silent.

Then David's dog grabbed

Stanley's pillowcase in his teeth

and began chewing it.

“Hey, cut that out!” cried Stanley,

yanking the pillowcase back.

“What’s in there?”

asked David.

“It’s stuff I need to run away.”

"Wow," said David.

"I wish I could run away."

"Don't you like it

at your house?"

Stanley asked.

"Not much," said David.

"My mother is always nagging."

Stanley looked
carefully at David.
"How would you like
to live someplace where
you'd be more appreciated?"
"Boy, would I!" said David.
"Where?"
"My house," said Stanley.
"Now that I've moved out,
you can have my room."

"And you can have my room,"

suggested David.

"Then it's a deal?"

"Deal."

Stanley and David shook hands

and went in

opposite directions.

In a few minutes

Stanley stood in front of

the Levine's door.

He knocked softly.

Mrs. Levine and

a wonderful smell

greeted him.

“Why, it’s my favorite violinist,”

she said.

“Come in and have

a blueberry muffin.”

Mrs. Levine gave Stanley

a muffin that was still hot

from the oven.

“This is delicious,”

said Stanley,

gobbling it down.

Then he cleared his throat.

"Mrs. Levine," he said,

"David has asked me

to speak to you. He's decided..."

"Don't tell me,"

interrupted Mrs. Levine.

"Let me guess.

I bet David has decided

to play the violin

and you're here to give him

his first lesson."

"Not exactly," said Stanley.

"Come on," said Mrs. Levine.

"You can't fool me.

I see the violin in your pillowcase.

And I know my David.

He wants to make his mother

as proud as you've made yours."

Stanley stared at Mrs. Levine.

"My mother's proud of me?"

he asked.

"What a question!"

said Mrs. Levine.

"All she talks about is

her Stanley."

"*Her* Stanley?"

"Who else?"

said Mrs. Levine.

Suddenly Stanley stood up.

"Mrs. Levine," he said,

picking up his pillowcase,

"I have to go."

And with that,

Stanley was out the door.

He ran and ran,

but he stopped when

he spotted David.

“Hey, David,” said Stanley,

out of breath,

“Did you see my mother?”

"I almost did," said David.

"I walked all the way

to your house and then

I remembered.

It's Sunday.

I can't run away on Sunday."

"Why not?" asked Stanley.

"Because my mother makes
her special fried chicken
on Sunday. I couldn't miss that."
"Phew," said Stanley.

“Want to come over for supper?”

asked David.

“We always have lots.”

“I can’t,” said Stanley,

and he dashed down

the street again.

Soon he was at his own front door.

It was open and he walked in.

He could hear his mother

on the phone.

"Helen," she was saying,

"have you seen my Stanley?"

Stanley tapped his mother

on the shoulder.

"Stanley!" she cried.

"You're home!"

With a quick goodbye

to her friend,

she hung up the phone.

“Where have you been, Stanley?”

she asked.

“I’ve called everyone

and I’ve been

worried sick.”

“You have?” asked Stanley.

“Of course,” said his mother.

“You’re my son and I love you.”

Stanley looked thoughtfully

at his mother.

"Would you still love me

if I didn't play the violin?"

he asked.

"Of course," said his mother.

"Would you still love me

if I failed math?"

"Of course," said his mother.

"Would you still love me
if I never *ever* folded my pants?"
Stanley's mother smiled and
put her arms around her son.
"I'd love you no matter what.
But why are you asking me
all these questions?"
"Just checking," said Stanley,
as he unpacked his pillowcase.